To Laura—

Best,

Dan G.

The Onts

☙ SECRETS OF ☙

DRIPPING FANG

BOOK ONE

The Onts

DAN GREENBURG

Illustrations by SCOTT M. FISCHER

HARCOURT, INC.

Orlando   Austin   New York   San Diego   Toronto   London

*I want to thank my editor, Allyn Johnston, for her macabre yet soulful
sense of humor, for her eagerness to explore ideas beyond the bounds of taste,
for understanding an author's poignant thirst for praise, and for helping
me say exactly what I'm trying to say, except more gooder.
I also want to thank Scott M. Fischer,
an artist with dizzying technical abilities and a demented genius
at combining terror and humor in the same illustration.*
—D. G.

Copyright © 2005 by Dan Greenburg

For information about permission to reproduce
selections from this book, please write Permissions,
Houghton Mifflin Harcourt Publishing Company
215 Park Avenue South NY NY 10003.
www.hmhbooks.com
Illustrations copyright © 2005 by Scott M. Fischer

Library of Congress Cataloging-in-Publication Data
Greenburg, Dan.
Secrets of Dripping Fang, book one: The Onts/
by Dan Greenburg; [illustrated by Scott M. Fischer].
p.   cm.
Summary: Ten-year-old orphan twins Wally and Cheyenne
Shluffmuffin have it bad at Cincinnati's Jolly Days orphanage,
but things get much worse when the Mandible sisters offer
to share their home in the Dripping Fang Forest.
[1. Orphans—Fiction.   2. Twins—Fiction.
3. Brothers and sisters—Fiction.   4. Swamps—Fiction.
5. Ants—Fiction.   6. Cincinnati (Ohio)—Fiction.]
I. Fischer, Scott M., ill.   II. Title.   III. Series.
PZ7.G8278Sec 2005
[Fic]—dc22   2004028493
ISBN-13: 978-0152-05457-1   ISBN-10: 0-15-205457-X

Text set in Meridien
Designed by Linda Lockowitz

DOC 10 9 8 7 6
4500395841

Printed in the United States of America

Contents

The Onts

CHAPTER 1

The Jolly Days Orphanage

The first thing Wally Shluffmuffin heard was the familiar crackle of the loudspeaker in the darkness. Next he heard the too-loud, too-cheery voice yell:

"Five a.m., orphans! Rise and shine!"

Wally couldn't believe it was five already. He didn't think he'd been asleep for more than an hour or two. Next he heard the too-loud tape of the rooster crowing.

"When the rooster crows, jump into your clothes!" yelled the voice on the loudspeaker.

Next he heard the too-loud bugle call that wakes soldiers in the army.

"Out of your sacks, troops!" yelled the voice

on the loudspeaker. "Chow in the mess hall in six minutes!"

This was the way Wally had to wake up every morning. He couldn't decide what he hated more—the stupid rooster, the stupid bugle, or the stupid yelling voice of stupid Hortense Jolly, owner of the stupid Jolly Days Orphanage of Cincinnati.

Thirty-eight orphans fell all over each other in the dark dorm, pulling on clothes. Still half asleep, Wally started dressing, stubbing his toes and putting his jeans on backward.

The dorm was a long room with mattresses on the floor. A rope divided the dorm. A scuzzy blanket hung from the rope, separating the boys' area from the girls'. Like most things at Jolly Days, the dorm smelled of hospital soap and the rotting carcasses of rats that had crawled into the walls, seeking better food than was being served in the orphanage, and died terrible deaths.

Wally knew he had just six minutes to dress, make his bed, race the other kids to the john, throw cold water on his face, drag a comb through his hair, squirt toothpaste in his mouth, and scramble to his place at the breakfast table.

Hortense Jolly waited in the dining hall with a stopwatch. Precisely six minutes after the bugle blew, she bonged a heavy brass bell with her soup ladle—*BONNNGGG!*

If you weren't in your seat when the bell bonged, you had to do extra chores.

Wet orphans with unbuttoned shirts and toothpaste smears on their faces tumbled into the dining room.

The bell bonged.

Wally ran in, tripped, and skidded across the dining room floor on his belly.

"Wally Shluffmuffin, you are precisely seven seconds late," Hortense Jolly announced. "As your reward you get to clean all the toilets!"

Wally groaned. He took the seat his sister, Cheyenne, had saved right next to her.

Wally and Cheyenne Shluffmuffin looked almost exactly alike. Both were ten years old.

Both had rust-colored hair, freckles on their cheeks and noses, and identical salami-shaped birthmarks on their left shoulders.

"I *hate* cleaning the toilets," whispered Wally to his sister.

"Why? The toilets are the cleanest things at Jolly Days," whispered Cheyenne.

Cheyenne saw only the good side of life, Wally only the bad. Cheyenne always saw a glass as half full, not half empty. Wally was sure a half-full glass had a leak that would ruin everything underneath it.

The Shluffmuffin twins had two flaws:

(1) Cheyenne was allergic to ragweed and roses and cats and dogs and dust and mold and milk and wheat and wool and soybeans and flour and everything else you could possibly be allergic to, so she was usually either sneezing or blowing her nose.

People around her had stopped saying "God bless you" or "Gesundheit" every time she sneezed, because it was taking up all of their time.

(2) There is no polite or pleasant way to say

5

this, so here it is: Wally's feet just plain stank. No matter how often he washed them, scrubbed them, sprayed them with Lysol, or soaked them in vinegar or hot sudsy ammonia, his feet reeked worse than festering, maggoty meat.

But if you didn't count sneezing or foot stink, Cheyenne and Wally were model children.

"And now, orphans, please rise for The Song," said Hortense Jolly.

Hortense Jolly, who planned someday to write musicals for the Broadway theater, had composed "The Jolly Days Loyalty Song." Every morning the orphans had to stand and sing all four verses before they were allowed to eat.

The children struggled to their feet. Hortense Jolly marked time with her soup ladle, and they sang:

"Oh, an orphan's life is super, we have found,
With no moms or daddies bossing us around.
There's no better friend, by golly,
Than our precious Hortense Jolly—
We will love her till we're six feet underground!

"When we're eatin' steaks, they're always piping
hot!
Are we ever whipped or beaten? I think not!
No, Miss Jolly has a way
To make sure that we obey—
Do not think that she is dumb, because she's smott!

"If an orphan misbehaves, a siren's sounded.
If that orphan is found guilty, he is grounded.
If he's scolded, it's done sadly.
If he's spanked, it's not too badly.
And he's never held beneath the water till he's
drownded.

"Oh, our orphanage we love in many ways, §
But someday we hope to enter a new phase
With a brand-new mom or daddy
In a home in Cincinnati—
Though we'll puke our guts out, missing Jolly
Days."

The orphans took their seats again and began
their breakfast.

Breakfast was stale bread crusts and tea. Each orphan was allotted just one tea bag per month, so after the first few days the tea was only hot water with a faint memory of what was in the bag.

Lunch was a bowl of gruel—a thick gray soup that looked and tasted like mucus. Dinner was gruel with little green floaty things that were supposed to be broccoli but looked like boogers.

All orphans at Jolly Days grumbled about the food. All orphans but Cheyenne.

"I suppose you *like* eating mucus with boogers for dinner every night," said Wally to his sister.

"Oh, Wally, for heaven's sake, it's not mucus with boogers—Ah-CHOO! It's soup with broccoli," said Cheyenne. "And things here could be a whole lot worse."

"How could they possibly be worse?" Wally asked.

"Well—Ah-CHOOF!—we could be chained to the wall and forced to eat spiders," said Cheyenne.

"That could still happen," said Wally.

"Or there could be no Saturday Night Treat," said Cheyenne.

"Oh, right," said Wally bitterly. "What would we do without the fabulous Saturday Night Treat!"

Every Saturday night as a special treat, the orphans were allowed to share a Choco-Doodle-Doo chocolate bar. Because there were thirty-eight orphans at the Jolly Days Orphanage, a Choco-Doodle-Doo bar split thirty-eight ways gave each orphan a piece of chocolate the size of a pencil eraser.

Every day the orphans at Jolly Days had to do six hours of chores.

Every day they washed the dishes with boiling water. Every day they took large greasy pots and pans caked with baked-on brown crust and scoured them with steel wool.

Every day they washed the windows, chipped rust off the pipes with hammers and chisels, and cleaned the toilets with strong hospital soap.

Every day they made up the smelly beds, did

the stinky laundry, dusted, and mopped the sticky floors with ammonia.

At the end of each week, whichever orphan had done his chores the best won a prize. The prize was that he got to wax and polish Hortense Jolly's red-and-white 1956 Oldsmobile convertible.

None of the orphans had ever seen anybody ride in Hortense Jolly's red-and-white 1956 Oldsmobile convertible, not even Hortense Jolly herself. But the car was so shiny after all that waxing and polishing, you couldn't stare at it directly without hurting your eyes.

Jolly Days orphans did not go to school. Instead, Hortense Jolly had invented a home-study plan she felt was much better for them than anything taught in schools: She assigned each orphan a letter of the alphabet. Each orphan had to learn every word in the encyclopedia that started with his or her letter.

Wally got the *A*'s, Cheyenne the *S*'s. After a year of studying the *A*'s, Wally asked if he could possibly move on to another letter.

"That depends, Wally," said Hortense Jolly. "Do you know every single word in the encyclopedia that begins with *A*?"

"Yes, Miss Jolly," Wally answered.

"Okay, give me the definition of the word *abelmosk*."

" '*Abelmosk*,' " Wally repeated in a good strong voice. "A plant of the mallow family. Its seeds are used to make perfume."

"Good," said Hortense Jolly. "Okay, what's the definition of *axolotl*?"

" '*Axolotl*,' " Wally repeated. "A salamander found chiefly in Mexico and the western United States."

"Fine so far," said Hortense Jolly. "All right, Mr. Smarty-pants, tell me the definition of . . . *argala*."

" '*Argala*,' " Wally repeated. "An African stork, also know as the marabou."

"Not bad," said Hortense Jolly. "Now, what is the definition of *azedarach*?"

" '*Azedarach*'?" Wally repeated. "Uh . . . let me think."

Wally scratched his head and tried to remember the definition of *azedarach*.

Hortense Jolly chuckled nastily. "I thought you said you knew all your *A*'s," she taunted.

Wally began perspiring heavily. He really wanted to be through with the *A*'s. He was sick to death of the *A*'s. He knew the word *azedarach*. He had read it hundreds of times. *Thousands* of times. He just couldn't remember right that minute what it meant.

"Let me tell you the definition of *aye-aye*," said Wally, "which is right next to *azedarach* in the encyclopedia. An aye-aye is a kind of lemur found in Madagascar. It has shaggy brown fur, large ears, pointed claws, and a long bushy tail."

"I didn't *ask* you the definition of *aye-aye*, Wally," said Hortense Jolly. "I asked you the definition of *azedarach*. If you *really* knew your *A*'s, you would tell me that *azedarach* is the chinaberry tree, or its bark, which is used to make medicine. I suggest you *seriously* learn your *A*'s, young man."

Wally sighed and returned to his *A*'s.

CHAPTER 2

A Warm Jolly Days Welcome for Sniffles and Stinkfoot

The year they turned seven had been a bad year for the Shluffmuffin twins. The week of October 12 was particularly awful.

On Monday while visiting the Cincinnati circus, their father, Sheldon Shluffmuffin, a slender man, fell through the seat of a Porta Potti and drowned.

On Tuesday at the petting zoo, where she had taken the twins to get their minds off their father's death, their mother, Sharon Shluffmuffin, was overpowered and smothered by a gang of angry bunnies.

Luckily, nothing bad happened on Wednesday.

The twins' only remaining relative was tiny

Grandma Gloria Shluffmuffin, a ninety-eight-year-old lady who weighed just forty-nine pounds. On Thursday of that terrible week, while snoozing in her backyard and wearing a black sleep mask, Grandma Gloria was carried off by a nearsighted eagle that mistook her for a raccoon.

With no father, mother, or tiny grandma left to take care of them, the twins were trundled off to the Jolly Days Orphanage on the outskirts of Cincinnati, where they lived for the next three years. They missed their mom and dad and tiny grandma terribly. They longed to be taken care

of by somebody who loved them. They yearned to be adopted.

Shortly after the Shluffmuffin twins arrived at Jolly Days, a tall fat boy named Rocco tried to pin a rude nickname on Wally.

"Hey, Wally, you know what your new name is? It's Stinkfoot," he said. "Hey, everybody, say hello to Stinkfoot."

Several boys around them giggled, but Wally punched Rocco in the stomach and the name never stuck.

The following week Rocco tried it again, this time on Cheyenne.

"Hey, Cheyenne, I'm thinking of calling you either Sneezy or Sniffles," he said, "depending on which one you hate more. Which one do you hate more?"

Wally punched Rocco in the stomach again, and that pretty much ended the nickname experiment.

Couples who were thinking of adopting a child came by the Jolly Days Orphanage every

Monday to check out the latest crop of orphans. They would discuss the orphans' strong and weak points in front of them, as if the children couldn't hear:

"That one has a nose like an elephant," they'd say. Or "This one smells like monkey vomit." Or "That one has ears so big he could flap them and fly away."

At such times Hortense Jolly was quick to point out the orphans' *good* qualities.

"This one's as strong as a water buffalo," she'd say. "If you bought a piano, she could carry it up three flights of stairs to your apartment without you lifting a finger. That one's as tiny as a hummingbird. You could feed her for a week on six raisins and a cup of Cheerios."

Hortense Jolly would then pry open the children's jaws and show their teeth like horses'. "Just look at those molars," she'd say. "You could crack walnuts between those puppies. And look at these bicuspids. You could loosen up rusty bolts with them."

If an orphan was chosen, the couple could

take the child home for a free weeklong trial adoption. Then if the orphan was adopted, the adopting parents had to pay Hortense Jolly six hundred dollars.

Hortense Jolly loved it when an orphan was adopted. Every time that happened, she announced a celebration. Every child was allowed to sleep five minutes later in the morning, and at dinner every child was given a shiny new penny.

"We're all partners here at Jolly Days," Hortense Jolly would say on these occasions. "We're all members of the Jolly Days Team. I give you these shiny new pennies because I want to share my profits with you every time one of our precious orphans finds a new home."

"Some sharing," grumbled Wally. "She gets six hundred bucks, we get a penny."

"A penny here, a penny there—it all adds up," said Cheyenne.

Every once in a while, some couple would take Wally and Cheyenne home with them for a trial adoption. But no matter how adorable they tried to be, Wally and Cheyenne were always returned to the orphanage.

When Hortense Jolly asked why, the couples usually said: "Well, the girl is constantly sneezing and blowing her nose. And the boy's feet stink worse than barn animals."

Cheyenne tried awfully hard not to sneeze or blow her nose, but it was no use.

Wally washed his feet so often his skin peeled, but they still stunk to high heaven.

So Wally and Cheyenne resigned themselves to living at the orphanage until they grew old and had gray hair.

Then one Monday afternoon, two odd ladies appeared at Jolly Days—the Mandible sisters, Hedy and Dagmar. And the lives of Wally and Cheyenne Shluffmuffin would never again be the same.

CHAPTER 3

Orphans Are Not
Vacuum Cleaners

The Mandibles were bigger than most women—they were about six feet tall. They had very large heads. They wore black straw hats with wide brims and huge black sunglasses. They had long black gloves that went up to their elbows. They smelled funny—a kind of coppery, earthy smell.

"We're here to adopt some orphans," said the taller one, whose name was Dagmar Mandible.

"Boy, have *you* ever come to the right place," said Hortense Jolly. "We have more orphans than a kid has cooties. What sort of orphans were you looking for?"

"Do you have any with allergies?" asked Hedy Mandible.

"What kind of allergies did you have in mind?" asked Hortense Jolly suspiciously.

"Oh, you know," said Hedy. "Ragweed. Cats. Dust. Rotting corpses. The usual. Do you have anything like that?"

"We might," said Hortense Jolly. "Of course, they aren't *serious* allergies, and if the children take their allergy pills, you won't even know they have them."

"Well, that's a pity," said Dagmar Mandible. "Because we *were* looking for serious allergies. Really *terrible* allergies. Fill-up-fifty-tissues-a-day-with-snot allergies."

"I see," said Hortense Jolly. "And were there any other qualities that were important to you in a child you might wish to adopt?"

"Stinky feet," said Dagmar.

"The stinkier the better," Hedy added helpfully.

Hortense Jolly thought this over carefully before she replied.

"Are you people serious, or is this some kind of joke?" she asked in a nasty tone.

Dagmar leaned in so close to her that Hortense Jolly became frightened.

"I assure you, madam," said Dagmar in a steely voice, "neither my sister nor I *ever* joke about anything as serious as allergies or stinky feet."

"I meant no disrespect," said Hortense Jolly quickly. "And in that case, we do have two children who just might interest you. Twins, in fact."

Hortense Jolly scurried off to get Wally and Cheyenne before the Mandible sisters could change their minds. She found the Shluffmuffin twins on their knees, scrubbing the sticky black-and-white tiles on the bathroom floor with ammonia and boiling water.

"Come quickly, Shluffmuffins," she said. "There are two adopters in the visiting room who want to see you. This could be our lucky day!"

"Oh, right. Like anybody is ever going to want to adopt *us*," said Wally sarcastically.

"Maybe they will, Wally," said Cheyenne hopefully. "You never can tell. Oh, I would *so* love a new set of parents!"

"It's not going to happen, sis," said Wally, "so forget about it."

Hortense took the twins into the visiting room.

"These are the Shluffmuffin twins, Cheyenne and Wally," said Hortense.

"Hello, children," said Dagmar Mandible.

"Hello, darlings," said Hedy Mandible.

"Glad to meet you!" said Cheyenne brightly, suddenly grabbing her nose to stifle a sneeze.

"Howya doin'," said Wally without any enthusiasm.

The Mandible sisters looked the twins over carefully from all angles. They pinched their cheeks and arms. They squatted down and peered up their nostrils. They bent down and sniffed their feet.

Cheyenne tried to keep from sneezing, but it was no use. "Ah-CHOO! Ah-CHOW! Ah-CHUFF!" She sneezed six times and blew her nose loudly into a tissue. When she went to throw the tissue away, Hedy grabbed her tightly by the wrist.

"Here, let me throw that away for you, precious," Hedy whispered. She took the tissue from Cheyenne, but instead of throwing it into the trash, she slipped it into her purse.

"These children do seem rather skinny," said Dagmar Mandible. "What's the matter, Miss Jolly, don't you feed them?"

"Madam," said Hortense Jolly in a proud tone, "our chef feeds these orphans only the finest of gourmet meals. Scrumptious milk-fed veal in a buttery lemon sauce. Crispy fried chicken that's finger-lickin' good. Taste-tempting porterhouse steaks, charbroiled to perfection. And for dessert? Delectable puff pastries filled with whipped cream and drizzled with blackberry syrup. I swear," she chuckled, "you'd think you were in the main dining room of the Cincinnati Ramada Inn!"

Wally looked at Cheyenne and rolled his eyes. Cheyenne had to bite her tongue to keep from laughing. Then she sneezed a seventh time.

"If you feed them that well, then why are they so skinny?" asked Hedy Mandible.

"Well, their father was skinny," said Hortense Jolly. "It runs in the family. Has nothing to do with how they're fed. If you like, I can show you something fatter. We do carry the heavier models."

"Never mind," said Dagmar. "These two will do just fine. Pack them up and we'll take them home for the free trial period."

"Pack them up?" Hortense Jolly repeated.

"You know," said Dagmar. "Get together all the stuff they come with."

"These are orphans, not vacuum cleaners," said Hortense Jolly. "They do not come with attachments. What you see is what you get."

"Fine," said Dagmar. "We'll take them as is."

"Here's your paperwork," said Hortense Jolly, handing Dagmar a sheaf of legal papers. "The trial period is a week. If they disappoint you in any way, simply return them, no questions asked. This week only, we're having a two-for-one sale: Adopt one orphan for six hundred dollars, get the second orphan free."

Wally and Cheyenne pulled together their only personal belongings—their toothbrushes, their second pairs of underpants, the plastic salt-and-pepper shaker given to Cheyenne by tiny Grandma Gloria, and the Boy Scout knife given to Wally by his dad—and they left with the Mandible sisters.

Cheyenne and Wally didn't much like the Mandible sisters. To tell you the truth, the Mandible sisters totally creeped them out. But the twins were desperate to be adopted. And they figured anything was better than the Jolly Days Orphanage.

They could not have been more wrong.

CHAPTER 4

Cincinnati, City of Mystery

Cincinnati may not sound like a scary place, but there's much in the area that is frightening. For example, Cincinnati is in Ohio, yet when you fly to Cincinnati, you find that the airport isn't in Ohio at all—it's in Kentucky. Some people find this frightening.

Not far from Cincinnati is Wright-Patterson Air Force Base. After the UFO crash of 1947 in Roswell, New Mexico, the little alien bodies found inside the UFOs were secretly flown to Wright-Patterson Air Force Base and stored in Hangar 18.

The Air Force has always denied that there were little alien bodies stored in Hangar 18, or that there even *is* a Hangar 18. To this day three Air Force generals deny that there's a Wright-Patterson Air Force Base, and one of them denies that there's a Cincinnati.

In the woods near Cincinnati, there are frequent sightings of a creature known as Moth Man. Moth Man has been described as a fellow about six feet tall with large glowing red eyes and the wings of a common clothes moth. He chases people through the woods, shrieking, flapping his enormous powdered wings, and trying to nibble their clothing.

Little is known about where Moth Man came from, but one legend tells of a Cincinnati math teacher named Arnold Mothman. He mistakenly ate 127 mothballs, believing them to be a new flavor of Reese's Pieces.

In the swamps near Cincinnati, people have recently seen a zombie sloshing through the shallow waters at night. He smells like rotting meat and is usually heard humming what some have identified as "Itsy bitsy spider climbed up the water spout."

Many people have gone to Cincinnati as tourists and were never heard from again. Some think of Cincinnati and its suburbs as the Bermuda Triangle of Ohio.

The cab ride from the Jolly Days Orphanage to the Mandible home took Dagmar, Hedy, and the Shluffmuffin twins out to the interstate highway and well beyond the city limits of Cincinnati.

After they'd traveled a good hour, the sun was low in the sky—orange and fat and ready to plop into the purple hills. The cab drew up before a dark wooded area and stopped. A dirt road led sharply off the main highway into the woods. Above the entrance to the woods was a tall archway and a sign that read: DRIPPING FANG FOREST.

"Dagmar, why is the driver stopping here?" asked Hedy Mandible.

"Driver, why are you stopping here?" asked Dagmar Mandible.

"This is as far as I go, ma'am," said the driver nervously.

31

"What do you mean this is as far as you go?" said Dagmar. "We aren't home yet."

"I know that, ma'am," said the driver, "but I make it a point never to go into Dripping Fang Forest."

"Why not?"

"I've heard way too many stories from other drivers, ma'am," said the driver. "Stories about . . . well, about things that live in there."

"What kind of things?" Dagmar demanded.

"Bad things, ma'am. Vines that reach out, grab you, and strangle the breath out of you. Slimy gray ten-foot-long giant slugs that glow in the dark, attach themselves to your legs, and suck the feet right off your ankles. Man-eating wolves who speak and say rude things."

"Whatever you've heard is nonsense," said Dagmar. "We *live* in Dripping Fang Forest. And we've never seen anything like strangling vines or giant slugs in there. Not ever."

"I don't care, ma'am," said the driver. "I got a wife and kids. They depend on me to come home every night in one piece, with the right number of hands and feet. For *their* sakes I'm not going in them there woods."

Dagmar sighed an irritated sigh.

"Oh, for the love of heaven," she said.

She opened her purse and took out some bills with her black-gloved hands.

She counted her money, and then Wally—he couldn't be sure of this because it happened so fast—thought he saw two more black-gloved hands dart out of slits in the waist of Dagmar's dress, drop some coins into the gloved hand holding the bills, and disappear back into the waist of her dress.

"Did you see that?" Wally hissed in his sister's ear.

"Did I see what?" whispered Cheyenne.

"She has four hands," whispered Wally.

"She has four *what*?" whispered Cheyenne.

"What are you children whispering about?" asked Dagmar.

"Nothing," said Cheyenne.

"If you're going to whisper, dears, please do it out loud," said Hedy.

"If we did it out loud, it wouldn't be whispering," said Wally.

"Don't be fresh, Walter," said Dagmar.

Wally and Cheyenne looked around them.

On one side of the highway were scruffy-looking businesses. A service station with rusty gas pumps. A store that sold rusty lawn furniture and rusty iron beds. A warehouse that sold stacks of old tires with worn-out treads. A shop that repaired rusty trucks. An empty lot strewn with rusty lawn furniture, old tires, and parts of rusty trucks.

On the other side of the highway was Dripping Fang Forest. The forest was so thick and so dark it seemed to swallow up light like a black hole.

Next to the sign that read DRIPPING FANG FOREST was a smaller sign. It read: PRIVATE PROPERTY. KEEP OUT. THIS MEANS YOU. TRESPASSERS WILL BE ...

The word PROSECUTED had been crossed out and somebody had written SHOT above it. The word SHOT had been crossed out, and somebody had written TORN APART BY WOLVES above that.

"I don't get a good feeling about this place," said Wally.

"Why, because of what that stupid cab driver said?" asked Dagmar.

"Yeah, and things like this sign," said Wally.

"Now, precious, don't pay any attention to that silly sign," said Hedy. "That's just the neighborhood kids playing their mischievous little tricks."

"Oh, do a lot of kids live in Dripping Fang Forest?" asked Cheyenne hopefully. "Ah-CHOOF!"

"Oh my, yes," said Hedy, swiftly mopping Cheyenne's nose with a tissue and snapping it into her purse. "Yes indeedy. A lot of kids. A whole lot. Well, a few, anyway."

"A few?" said Cheyenne.

"A few," said Hedy. "Well, one in particular. A boy named Alvin. Alvin Ailing. Lovely boy. A bit sickly, but lovely. Although, come to think of it, even *he* might be gone by now."

"What happened to him?"

"Just . . . went away, I think," said Hedy. "Nobody really knows. Some say he got more and more blurry every day, then just went completely out of focus. Come, my darlings, let us proceed."

The Mandible sisters led the way into the forest. After a few blocks the dirt road trickled down to a narrow trail. It was hard to see how a cab could have driven any farther, even if the driver had not been too frightened to try.

After the twins entered Dripping Fang Forest, things felt different. For one thing it was at least fifteen degrees cooler. And the soft ground was covered by clouds of cottony mist.

"I love the woods," said Cheyenne. "It's so quiet."

"I hate the woods," said Wally. "It's so quiet."

"I can feel my heart beating," said Cheyenne.

"I can feel things watching me," said Wally.

Wally was right. At this moment several things *were* watching them. One of these was a slimy gray ten-foot-long giant slug. If it had been nighttime, they would have seen it glowing unpleasantly in the dark.

Mmm, thought the giant slug, *orphans. Orphans with tasty feet. It has been such a long time since I have dined on the tasty feet of orphans. Much too long a time.*

"Mmm," said Hedy, "do you smell that wonderful moist earth smell? It smells just like it does after a sudden summer rain."

Wally and Cheyenne smelled the moist earth smell. They felt the sponginess of the ground under their feet as they walked. They listened to the chirping of the crickets, the ratcheting of the cicadas.

"I just love the sound of bugs in the forest," said Cheyenne.

"You might want to check your arms and legs for ticks," said Wally. "You wouldn't want to come down with Lyme disease. First you develop a rash that looks like a target, then you die."

The wind sighed through Dripping Fang Forest.

"Listen to the gentle noises of the woods,

37

children," said Hedy. "Do you hear the moaning of the wind? It sounds almost like a wounded animal, doesn't it?"

"Actually, that *is* a wounded animal," said Dagmar.

"If only we knew where it was," said Hedy dreamily, "perhaps we could...help it. Sadly, though, we don't."

It might not be such a good idea to attack them now, thought the giant slug. *There are too many of them, and it could get messy. The strangled screams. The thrashing about. The spattering of blood. The heartbreaking calls for help.*

No, I shall bide my time. I shall slither after them in the underbrush and wait for a better moment. Then, when the time is right, I shall dine on the tasty feet of orphans once again. Yum, delish!

Cheyenne, Wally, Dagmar, and Hedy walked farther into the forest. Occasionally they caught sight of a house through the tangle of trees and vines. It was hard for Cheyenne and Wally to tell if the houses they saw were occupied or abandoned.

Wally strayed from the path. He didn't notice the gigantic spiderweb that was stretched across his path like a delicate fairy volleyball net, and he walked smack into it. He shuddered and began picking the sticky strands out of his eyes and mouth and hair.

"What's wrong, Wally?" Cheyenne asked.

"Oh, I just walked into some stupid spiderweb," said Wally. "Yuck!"

"Spiderwebs are wonderful," said Cheyenne, helping him remove strands of it. "They're so strong. Did you know that, for its size, spider's silk is stronger than steel?"

"Did you know that the most poisonous spider in the whole country is the black widow, and the best place to find one is right here in southern Ohio?" said Wally, still picking web out of his hair. "Its venom is fifteen times more poisonous than a rattlesnake's."

"Come along, children," said Dagmar. "We have to hurry. The sun will set in less than thirty minutes. We must get through the woods and into our home before the sun goes down."

"Why? What happens after the sun goes down?" asked Wally.

Dagmar and Hedy looked at each other before they spoke.

"It's just better if we're inside after dark," said Dagmar.

CHAPTER 5

Mandible House Rules

The Mandible home was tucked into a far corner of Dripping Fang Forest. It was a once-magnificent old two-story building with a tower. It had pointed arches above the windows. The brown paint that had covered its shingles was peeling away in curled-up strips, like dead skin after a painful sunburn.

The house didn't look very inviting. And when they got up close, Wally and Cheyenne got a nasty surprise.

"There are *bars* on the windows!" cried Wally. "Why are there *bars* on the windows? Are you afraid we'll escape?"

"No, precious," said Hedy. "The bars aren't to keep anyone inside from getting out. The bars are to keep anyone *outside* from getting *in.*"

"Who are you trying to keep from getting in?" he asked.

"Any . . . uninvited guests," said Dagmar.

"We just don't like drop-in visitors," Hedy explained. "We like to have yummy snacks ready when people come to visit. But if we have no warning that they're coming, we can't do it. That's all."

Hedy unlocked the front door, and everybody went inside. The door slammed shut with a sound that echoed throughout the house.

The first thing that struck the twins about the inside of the house was the smell. The same kind of coppery, earthy smell as that of the Mandible sisters, only stronger.

The second thing that struck the twins about the inside of the house was the cleanliness. The Mandible house was the cleanest house they had ever seen. The floors were heavily waxed and polished, and looked clean enough to eat off. Wally didn't see a dining table anywhere and wondered if they *would* have to eat off the floor.

"Welcome to Mandible House," said Hedy. "We trust your time here will be merry and full of fun. And now my sister, Dagmar, will instruct you in the Mandible House Rules. Dagmar?"

"Thanks, Hedy," said Dagmar. "All right, children, rule number one: You will always address us as Aunt Dagmar and Aunt Hedy. And, notice, children, that we pronounce *Aunt* as *ONT,* not *ANT.*"

"That's because Dagmar and I are not insects," said Hedy. "Ha-ha."

"Ha-ha," said Dagmar. "If we do decide to adopt you, then—and *only* then—you may address us as Mommy Dagmar and Mommy Hedy. Understood? Good. So, to review, Cheyenne, how will you address us during the trial period?"

"Ont Dagmar and Ont Hedy," said Cheyenne. "Ah-CHOOF!"

Hedy swiftly mopped Cheyenne's nose and stuffed the tissue into her purse.

"Excellent, dear," said Dagmar. "And Walter, how will *you* address us during the trial period?"

"Ont Dagmar and Ont Hedy," said Wally.

"Excellent, Walter," said Dagmar. "Now then. Rule number two: Never at any time—and I can't stress this too strongly, children—*never* will you be permitted to go into either our bedrooms or the cellar. Is that quite clear? Cheyenne?"

"Yes, ma'am," said Cheyenne.

"Excuse me?" said Dagmar. "Yes, *what*?"

"Yes, *Ont Dagmar*," said Cheyenne. "Ah . . . ah-CHOWF!"

"Excellent," said Dagmar. "Walter, what is it that you children are never permitted to do?"

Wally swallowed and took a deep breath to control himself. "Go into your bedrooms or the cellar, Ont Dagmar," said Wally.

"Perfect, Walter," said Dagmar. "Rule number three: Any and all unusual noises or odors that you may notice in Mandible House are none of your business and are never to be asked about. Is that quite understood? Cheyenne?"

"Yes, Ont Dagmar," said Cheyenne.

"Good," said Dagmar. "Walter, would you kindly repeat house rule number three?"

Wally stifled a sigh. "Rule number three: Any and all unusual noises or odors that we may notice in Mandible House are none of our business and are never to be asked about."

"Absolutely fantastic, Walter," said Dagmar. "I am very impressed. Next, rule number four: Never, under any circumstances, will you ever tell anybody what you see or hear in Mandible House. Please repeat. Cheyenne?"

"Rule number four," said Cheyenne. "Never, under any circumstances, will we ever—Ah-CHERFF!—tell anybody what we see or hear in Mandible House."

"Perfect," said Dagmar. "Walter?"

"I have just one question about rule number three," said Wally. "The part about the unusual noises or odors?"

"Did I say that you could ask questions about

the Mandible House Rules, Walter?" said Dagmar. "Is that what I said?"

"No, Ont Dagmar," said Wally.

"That's what *I* thought, too," said Dagmar. "Now kindly repeat rule number four."

"Rule number four," said Wally. "Never, under any circumstances, will we ever tell anybody what we see or hear in Mandible House."

"If you remember just one rule—and, ha-ha, you'd better remember more than that—make it rule number four," said Dagmar. "And now a special treat to welcome you two lovely children, whom we hope someday to be able to call our own son and daughter."

Wally shuddered to think of someday being called Hedy and Dagmar's own son. Then he shuddered a second time to think what the special welcoming treat might be.

To his great surprise, the special treat was two banana splits with chocolate ice cream, whipped cream, and chocolate syrup. The children fell upon the banana splits and gobbled them up so fast, their teeth ached from the cold.

Then the Onts took Wally and Cheyenne upstairs to show them their rooms.

To the twins' continued surprise, the two bedrooms that the Onts had given them were charming. Each room had its own oak bed with several puffy pillows and a colorful quilt. Each room had its own oak dresser with mirror.

Not only that, but each room had its own color TV with extra cable channels, a laptop computer, and a PlayStation for video games.

"This is amazing!" cried Cheyenne. "I love it!"

"This is . . . very nice," said Wally. "I like it."

"A bit better than the Jolly Days Orphanage, isn't it?" said Hedy.

Both Wally and Cheyenne laughed out loud.

At the Jolly Days Orphanage, they had slept on the bare floor or on flat stained mattresses that smelled of pee. On cold nights they covered up with soiled Bubble Wrap. Instead of a TV there was a staticky radio that broadcast only weather reports for lower Ohio. There were never any games, except on nights that the orphans caught enough cockroaches to race them.

"All right," said Dagmar. "Dinner is promptly at seven. Relax, watch a little TV, but please come downstairs at six fifty-eight."

As soon as the Onts went downstairs, Cheyenne turned to Wally.

"So, what do you think of the Mandible sisters *now*?" she asked.

"I don't know," he replied.

"What don't you know?" she said. "Have we ever had anything like this before, Wally? Even when Mom and Dad were alive?"

"No, but..."

"But what?" asked Cheyenne.

"Well, there are things about the Onts that worry me."

"Like what?" asked Cheyenne.

"Like the fact that Dagmar seems to have an extra set of hands, for one thing," said Wally. "That's what I was trying to tell you when we got out of the cab."

"What makes you think she has an extra set of hands?" asked Cheyenne.

"I'm pretty sure I saw them dart out of her dress with some change for the cab driver."

"You're not positive, though, right?"

"Right," said Wally.

"Even if she *did* have an extra set of hands," said Cheyenne, "that wouldn't make her a bad person, would it?"

"I guess not," said Wally. "But there are other things."

"Like what?"

"Like the way they look," said Wally. "The size of their heads. And did you see what Hedy did with the Kleenexes you blew your nose in?"

"She threw them away for me."

"She put them in her purse," said Wally.

"Are you sure?"

"I'm positive, Cheyenne. I saw her do it. She put as many as she could in her purse. What does she want with your snotty tissues?"

"I don't know, Wally."

"I don't know, either," said Wally, "but it

creeps me out. And what's the deal with the bars on the windows and the having to be in before sundown?"

"Maybe they're just extra careful about safety."

"And what about those Mandible House Rules?" said Wally. "About never going into the cellar? About any noises or smells we may notice being none of our business? About being forbidden to even discuss them? About never telling anybody what we see or hear in the house?"

"Maybe they're just very private people."

"Yeah," said Wally. "Maybe that's it. Maybe they're just 'very private people.'"

Cheyenne thought about the Mandible sisters and smiled. "Who do you like better, Hedy or Dagmar?" she asked.

"I don't like either one of them," said Wally.

"I like Hedy the best," said Cheyenne. "I like how she calls us 'darling' and 'precious.' I think they're starting to like us already, Wally. I think they may actually adopt us."

"I really hope they don't," said Wally.

At 6:58 p.m., Wally and Cheyenne went downstairs for dinner. They didn't have to eat off the floor. There was, in fact, a regular dining table and a tablecloth and plates and silverware. In the middle of the table was a beautiful bunch of tiny yellow flowers in a blue glass vase.

The main course at dinner was a bittersweet Belgian chocolate layer cake with mocha frosting. Dessert was a double chocolate-fudge sundae with chocolate-flavored whipped cream and chocolate sprinkles.

Cheyenne would have enjoyed dinner even more if she could have sneezed less. Wally counted 336 sneezes between the chocolate dinner-mint appetizers that began the meal and the Yoo-hoo chocolate drinks that ended it. And then Cheyenne realized something.

"Are dose fwowers wagweed?" asked Cheyenne, her nose too stuffed for her to speak clearly. "Ah-CHOOF! Ah-CHOWF! Ah-CHERFF!"

"What, precious?" said Hedy.

Cheyenne blew her nose into her forty-third

tissue of the evening. Hedy snatched the tissue as she had all the others, and dropped it into a stainless-steel container under the table that clanked when it shut.

"I said . . . are those flowers ragweed?" Cheyenne repeated, mopping her nose with tissue number forty-four.

"Which flowers, precious?" Hedy asked, whisking the tissue out of Cheyenne's hand and slipping it into the airtight stainless-steel container.

"Those," said Cheyenne, pointing to the blue glass vase. "Ah-CHOWW!"

Hedy and Dagmar looked at the vase of flowers as if seeing it for the first time.

"My heavens," said Dagmar, frowning. "It certainly does *look* like ragweed. But why would anybody put a bouquet of ragweed on the dinner table, knowing how allergic poor Cheyenne is?"

"Yes," said Hedy, "that is the question, isn't it?"

"Perhaps," said Dagmar, "and I know this sounds far-fetched—perhaps some truly nasty person snuck in here and left it on the table while we weren't looking."

"But why would anybody do such a heartless thing?" asked Hedy.

CHAPTER 6

Breaking Rule Number Two

"The way I see it," said Cheyenne, "the all-chocolate dinner was the Onts' way of trying to please us."

They were in Cheyenne's room, lying on her bed and watching TV.

"The way *I* see it," said Wally, "the all-chocolate dinner was the Onts' way of trying to fatten us up so they can eat us."

"What I didn't like was when Hedy kept throwing my snotty Kleenexes into that special airtight container under the table," said Cheyenne.

"What *I* didn't like was when they asked me

to sleep with plastic Baggies tied around my feet," said Wally. "Why do you think they're doing these things?"

Cheyenne shook her head. "I don't know, Wally," she said. "Maybe they just want to keep your feet from stinking up their house. The Onts are very strange. But they seem harmless. And they *are* being very nice to us. I guess it couldn't hurt to do what they ask."

The twins watched cartoons in Cheyenne's room until she got tired. Then they said good night, and Wally went to his own room.

He turned off his light and lay in bed, thinking.

Things in Mandible House were sure better than they'd been at the Jolly Days Orphanage. Wally loved having his very own bedroom. And even if the Onts were weird and smelled funny, it's true they were being very nice.

But no matter how nice the Onts were acting now, Wally didn't trust them. If he and Cheyenne were in danger here, he had to find out while there was still time to do something about it.

Wally crept to the door of his bedroom and peered into the darkened hallway.

There was that strange coppery, earthy smell in the hallway. There was an odd sound—like *Ch-ch-ch-ch-ch . . . Ch-ch-ch-ch-ch*—coming from downstairs. And from somewhere nearby came the muffled voices of the Onts.

As quietly as he could, Wally crept forward.

The door to Dagmar's bedroom was slightly open, and a thin triangle of light lay across the hallway floor. Wally could hear voices inside the bedroom, but it was hard to make out what they were saying.

". . . and the babies will be pleased," said one of the voices.

". . . do think the babies will be *so* pleased," said the other.

Who were these babies they were talking about—Wally and Cheyenne? Wally and Cheyenne were ten years old. They were certainly *not* babies. And what would they be so pleased about? Were the Onts planning more all-chocolate dinners?

". . . should see real growth now very soon," said the first voice.

". . . can't wait to see the joy on their tiny faces," said the other.

Did Wally and Cheyenne have tiny faces? Well, maybe if you compared them to the giant heads of Dagmar and Hedy.

Wally shifted his weight and a floorboard creaked beneath his feet.

Immediately the voices stopped.

". . . you hear something?" whispered one.

". . . a floorboard," whispered the other.

Footsteps walked up to the bedroom door.

"Walter?" called a voice. It was Dagmar. "Cheyenne? Is that you?"

Wally tried to flatten himself out against the wall so that he might not be seen if either stuck a head into the darkened hallway.

"Aren't you children in bed yet?" Dagmar called.

Wally held his breath.

"I don't hear an answer," Dagmar whispered. "But I could swear somebody is out there. I *smell* somebody, Hedy."

Hedy whispered something to Dagmar, but Wally couldn't make it out.

"Well then, I'll have a look," Dagmar answered.

Oh no, thought Wally, *don't come out here! Please don't come out here now!*

As quietly as he could, Wally crept down the hallway in the direction away from his bedroom before Dagmar could come after him. Had she followed him? He couldn't tell.

He reached the end of the hallway. A flight of stairs. He crept silently down the stairs to the first floor and hid beneath the stairway. He heard Dagmar's footsteps on the landing above his head.

"Walter? Cheyenne?" called Dagmar from the second floor. "Are you kids still awake?"

Please don't come downstairs, thought Wally. *Please do not come downstairs!*

"It's completely quiet out here, Hedy," said Dagmar. "I think the children are asleep."

Wally heard Dagmar walk back into the bedroom.

Whew! That was close, he thought.

Under the stairway was a door. Above it was a sign. From the faint light coming in through the barred windows he could make out the words: CELLAR. DO NOT ENTER.

Wally didn't want to go into the cellar. The twins had been strongly warned not to go in there. But he had to find out what the Onts were up to while there was still time.

So Wally opened the cellar door. He was surprised it wasn't locked. He walked through the doorway, and closed the door quietly behind him.

CHAPTER 7

The Badness Beneath the Stairs

The cellar was moist, clammy, and lit by a naked bulb hanging from the ceiling. The strange coppery, earthy smell was much stronger down here than upstairs.

The sound he had heard upstairs was much louder down here, too: *Ch-ch-ch-ch-ch . . . Ch-ch-ch-ch-ch . . .*

Wally crept carefully down the steep stone stairway, wet with slime, trying hard not to slip and fall.

The ceiling held a maze of old pipes. Some of them were wrapped in rotting burlap cloth. All of them dripped onto the stone floor, which was covered by at least two inches of water.

In the middle of the cellar stood an ancient furnace. Wally could clearly see a fire blazing deep within its firebox although it wasn't winter. Pipes and heating ducts ran from the furnace up to the ceiling.

Wally had been in the cellar of the Jolly Days Orphanage many times while doing his chores, so everything in this cellar looked somewhat familiar to him, even the water.

Everything, that is, but the two large machines along the back wall, and what looked like the world's largest egg cartons. The egg cartons couldn't have stood more than two feet off the ground, but they stretched across the floor of the cellar.

Wally sloshed along the floor to the two machines, aware his sneakers were getting soaked. Unlike the furnace, which was brown with rust, these machines were made of gleaming stainless steel.

One machine was tall and narrow. It had a huge glass bubble on the top. Out of its side came a long plastic tube, like the hose from a vacuum cleaner, with a large funnel at the end.

The other machine was low and flat. It looked like a stainless-steel toaster oven with a little window. Through the window Wally could see greenish-gray liquid.

A small nameplate at the top of the first machine read: ODOR EXTRACTOR.

Odor extractors draw the fragrance out of flowers to make perfume, Wally knew.

A similar nameplate at the top of the second machine read: SLOT PRESS.

What the heck is a Slot Press? Wally wondered. *No, wait a minute. That isn't an L, it's an N—not* SLOT PRESS, *but* SNOT PRESS!

Suddenly Wally knew what these machines were made to do—extract foot odor from plastic Baggies and squeeze the mucus out of snot-filled Kleenexes! And the greenish-gray liquid that filled the tank was snot.

Ugh! Wally thought. *What in the world do the Onts want with such disgusting things?*

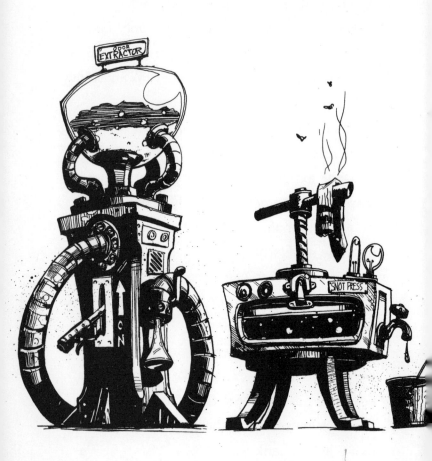

Next Wally peeked into the egg cartons that stretched across the floor of the cellar. They held dozens—no, *hundreds*—of compartments, each the size of a Chihuahua puppy.

Moving closer, Wally saw that each and every compartment in the egg carton held something alive.

Not Chihuahua puppies.

They looked like giant caterpillar cocoons, and they were open at the top. Inside each compartment was something sickening—a slimy gray creature with no eyes and a quivering open mouth. It was the creatures' mouths that were making the *Ch-ch-ch-ch-ch* sounds Wally had heard before.

Yargh! Wally thought. For a moment he feared he was going to puke up his entire all-chocolate dinner.

The Onts are raising these horrible creatures in secret! he thought. *But why? And what do they have to do with the Odor Extractor and the Snot Press?*

Wally needed to get out of the cellar and

breathe. He needed to tell Cheyenne what he'd found. Just let her try to explain how this was nothing to worry about!

He sloshed his way across the floor and back to the cellar stairs, beginning to dread what was waiting for him upstairs.

CHAPTER 8

The Truth About the Onts

Just before he opened the cellar door, Wally had a sudden terrifying image—an image of the Onts ready to pounce.

What would he do if he met up with them now? How would he explain why he went into the cellar when they had clearly forbidden him to do so?

Luckily, nobody was waiting for him upstairs. The house was absolutely dark and silent.

Wally shut the cellar door behind him and crept slowly up to the second floor.

When he got to the upstairs hallway, he could still see the narrow band of light coming from Dagmar's bedroom. He crept closer, but he could no longer hear the voices. Perhaps Hedy had gone to her own room.

Wally crept closer still. Another yard or two, and he could peer through the open crack in the door.

He crouched on the floor, placing one hand carefully in front of him. Then he slowly shifted his weight and placed his other hand in front of the first. Now he could stretch his neck forward. Now he could see into Dagmar's bedroom. And what he saw was . . .

A table.

A table with some pieces of clothing on it. A wide-brimmed black hat. Several pairs of long black gloves. A pair of large black sunglasses. Something pink and rubbery.

What was the pink rubbery thing? Wally looked closer. It looked almost like a mask. Yes, a mask. A pink rubber Halloween mask!

He again put a hand on the floor in front of him and crawled another step forward. If he just stuck his neck out a little farther, he could get a whole different angle on the room.

He stretched forward. He couldn't see either Dagmar or Hedy. And then he heard somebody. Somebody in the bedroom closet. Somebody coming out of the bedroom closet.

It wasn't Dagmar Mandible.

It wasn't Hedy Mandible.

It was . . .

It was a giant ant, six feet tall and walking on its hind legs!

It was the most disgusting thing Wally had ever seen in his life!

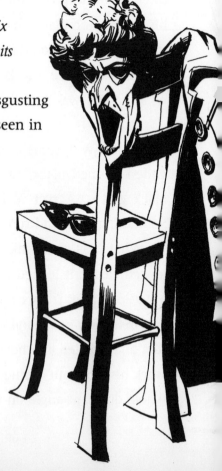

CHAPTER 9

Bad News and Worse News

Cheyenne awoke through several layers of sleep to find somebody shaking her roughly by the shoulders. It was Wally.

"Wally, what are you doing?" asked Cheyenne. "What time is it? Good grief, it must be the middle of the night! What's going on?"

Wally went to the door and peeked nervously out into the hallway. Then he quietly closed the door, locked it, and went back into the room.

"Cheyenne," said Wally, "I have bad news and worse news. What do you want to hear first?"

"I don't know," said Cheyenne. "Is the bad news really better than the worse news?"

"It's better. Definitely better," said Wally.

Cheyenne sighed. "Then tell me the bad news first," she said.

"Okay, Cheyenne. The bad news is we have been adopted by giant ants."

"I see," said Cheyenne. "Why do you think that?"

"Because I saw one of them without her hat and sunglasses and gloves and pink rubber human-face mask. And I saw her six legs and her huge black claws and her horrible head with her gigantic black eyes, and her horrible mouth that looks like a huge pair of horrible black pliers, only sharper. That's why."

Cheyenne took a moment to let what Wally was telling her sink in. "Wally, it's very late," she said. "You just had a nightmare."

"Cheyenne, this wasn't any nightmare. I really saw it. A six-foot-tall giant ant. You've got to believe me."

"Look, Wally, you say you saw a rubber mask on the table, right?" she asked.

"Of a human face," said Wally. "So?"

"So maybe what you thought was a giant ant was only Dagmar or Hedy wearing a giant ant *mask*. And a giant ant *costume*."

"Cheyenne, you've got to believe me. What I just saw was no costume. It was *real*."

Cheyenne looked at Wally for several seconds before answering him. She had never seen him so upset in her entire life.

"Okay," she said, "so Dagmar and Hedy are giant ants. That doesn't have to be a *bad* thing."

"How could it *not* be a bad thing?" Wally asked.

"Well," said Cheyenne, "they could teach us so much about their culture. About ant colonies and stuff. Just think what terrific grades we'd get in science class if we did an extra-credit project on ants."

"We don't even *go* to school," said Wally.

"Well, if we ever did, it would be so cool," said Cheyenne. "Okay, what's the *worse* news?"

"The worse news is that the Onts are collecting my foot odors and your snot and using it to feed hundreds of giant ant larvae—ant babies—in the cellar."

"And how do you know this?" asked Cheyenne.

"I saw it, Cheyenne. I saw a machine called an Odor Extractor. I saw a machine called a Snot Press. And I saw cocoons with hundreds of ant larvae the size of Chihuahua puppies. Slimy, pulsing, sickening-looking puppies with no eyes and quivering mouths. Remember I had to study all the *A* words? Well, one of my words was *ant*. So I know a whole lot about ants, Cheyenne. I know that ants talk to each other by using odors. And I know that ants feed their larvae the body fluids of other creatures. That's why they're feeding the larvae your snot."

Cheyenne took a deep breath. Then she closed her eyes. Then she let the air out.

"Okay, what if you're right, Wally?" she said. "What if everything you said is true? Why is that so terrible?"

"Why is that so terrible? I'll tell you why. Because they're growing a race of super-ants that will eventually make slaves out of the human race and end life on Earth as we know it, that's why."

"Why do you think super-ants would make slaves out of the human race?" she asked.

"What *else* do you think super-ants are going to do? You think super-ants are going to take orders from humans? You think they're going to treat us like equals? They're going to make *slaves* of us, Cheyenne. That's what super-ants *do.*"

"So what you're saying is . . ."

"What I'm saying, Cheyenne, is—*Let's get out of here now!*"

Cheyenne thought this over. It's true that she always tried to look on the bright side of things, but Cheyenne was not a moron. She sighed.

"Wally, I agree that we should get out of here now," said Cheyenne. "But how?"

"We'll just quietly creep downstairs, being careful not to wake the Onts," said Wally. "Then we're out the front door."

"And we're home free!" said Cheyenne.

"No, then we're out the door in the middle of Dripping Fang Forest after dark," said Wally.

Cheyenne frowned.

"Wally, do you really think we're going to find anything in Dripping Fang Forest worse than giant ants?" she asked.

"I'd bet big money on it," he said.

Just then there was a knock at Cheyenne's door.

Wally and Cheyenne froze in terror.

CHAPTER 10

Wally's Disobedience
Is Discovered

Cheyenne and Wally held their breaths.

There was another knock at the door.

Cheyenne turned to Wally, a questioning look on her face.

"Don't answer," Wally whispered.

"Cheyenne," said Dagmar's voice, "we know you're awake. Please open the door immediately."

Wally shook his head. Cheyenne remained silent.

For a moment nothing happened. Then they heard a key in the lock. The bedroom door clicked open.

There stood Hedy and Dagmar. They were wearing their human masks.

"We heard voices and we were worried," said Dagmar. "What are you children doing up so late?"

"Uh, we're just having a little trouble sleeping in a new house, I guess," said Wally.

"I see," said Dagmar. "We also noticed wet footprints all the way down the hallway."

Oh no, thought Wally. *I forgot about the wet footprints! How do I explain them?*

"I . . . took a shower," said Wally. "Sometimes I do that when I can't sleep. The hot water kind of relaxes me and makes me sleepy."

"Your sneakers are soaking wet, dear," said Hedy. "Don't tell me you showered in your sneakers."

I'm an idiot, thought Wally. *Why didn't I remember to take off my wet sneakers?*

"Uh yeah, as a matter of fact I did shower in my sneakers," said Wally. "See, I happen to have a terrible fear of athlete's foot. So I always wear my sneakers in the shower."

"The wet footprints start all the way down at the cellar door, Walter," said Dagmar.

"Oh," said Wally.

It's over, thought Wally miserably. *They know everything.*

"What is Mandible House rule number two, Walter?" asked Dagmar in a calm voice. "Do you remember Mandible House rule number two?"

"Uh, I don't exactly remember," said Wally. "Was that the one about the—"

"RULE NUMBER TWO!" Dagmar screamed. "NEVER AT ANY TIME WILL YOU BE PERMITTED TO GO INTO EITHER OUR BEDROOMS OR THE CELLAR! DO YOU REMEMBER THAT RULE, WALTER?"

"Uh, well, yeah, now that you mention it, I—"

"*SURELY* YOU DIDN'T GO INTO THE CELLAR AFTER HOW HARD WE WORKED WITH YOU ON RULE NUMBER TWO, WALTER!" Dagmar shouted. "*SURELY* YOU DIDN'T DO *THAT*?"

Wally gulped.

"Don't bother denying it, dear," said Hedy. "We know you've been down in the cellar. And we know that you've seen the babies."

Wally and Cheyenne looked at each other. For once Wally had no answer.

"Are you aliens from outer space?" he blurted.

"Aliens from outer space? I should say not!" said Dagmar in an offended tone. "We're Americans, good taxpaying Americans. And proud citizens of Cincinnati, Ohio, I might add."

"We vote in all national and local elections," said Hedy.

"We even have season tickets to all Cincinnati Reds home games," said Dagmar.

"If the Reds had even two strong starting pitchers, we think they might have a shot at the Wild Card," said Hedy.

"What are you growing in the cellar?" Wally demanded. "Are you breeding a race of super-ants to enslave humans and take over Earth?"

Dagmar and Hedy looked at each other and shrugged.

"Well, um, you know. Sort of," said Hedy.

"All right, what the heck," said Dagmar. "You've seen them, anyway, so we might as well tell you. We really are American citizens and we really do vote in all national and local elections—that part is true. But there are a few things we haven't been truthful about."

"First, my dears," said Hedy, "we are not fans of the Cincinnati Reds."

"We prefer the Cleveland Indians," said Dagmar. "We are not fools."

"Second, my darlings," said Hedy, "we were born not far from Cincinnati, in a cornfield where the farmer was using too much growth hormone."

"That's why we got to be so big," said Dagmar.

"Third, my sweethearts," said Hedy, "we *are* breeding a race of super-ants to enslave humans and take over Earth. We're feeding our little ant babies human foot odor and human snot, and it seems to be making them big and strong."

"You'll never get enough snot out of Cheyenne to do the job," said Wally, "no matter how many ragweed bouquets you put on the table."

Dagmar and Hedy chuckled.

"Oh, we know that," said Dagmar. "We have plans for getting lots more."

"We plan to get *tons* more snot by releasing a really awful cold virus in Cincinnati this winter, precious," said Hedy.

Hedy and Dagmar had a good laugh about that.

"I'll tell you what," said Wally, "if you let us go, we promise on our word of honor not to tell anybody about what you're doing here."

"Really?" said Hedy. "That is so *sweet*!"

"So will you let us go?" Wally asked.

"Most likely, darling," said Hedy. "Only not right now."

"But you aren't going to kill us, are you, Ont Hedy?" asked Cheyenne.

"Oh *no*, dear. Killing you won't be necessary," said Hedy. "I mean, you did promise not to tell anybody about us, didn't you?"

"Absolutely," said Wally.

Dagmar was exasperated.

"Hedy, you idiot. You don't really think we can let them go now, do you?" she snapped.

83

"But, Dagmar," said Hedy, "they promised not to tell anyone. On their word of *honor.*"

"Of *course* they promised not to tell anyone on their word of honor," said Dagmar. "What did you *expect* them to do?"

"Oh dear me," said Hedy. "I suppose you're right. Well, children, it seems I was wrong."

"What?" said Wally.

"It seems we're going to have to kill you after all," said Hedy.

"We're planning to kill you tomorrow morning," said Dagmar.

"We're going to have to get you chopped, boned, ground, and boiled into a yummy mush for the babies," Hedy explained. "But it won't hurt much, and it'll be over so fast you won't even know it. I'm so dreadfully sorry, my dears. I do hope you're not too disappointed."

Wally looked at Cheyenne. He could see she was terrified. He had never been so scared in his life, either. But he couldn't let his sister see how frightened he was. She counted on him to be strong. Grouchy and strong.

"When are you going to kill us?" Wally asked. "Now?"

"Oh, good heavens, no!" said Dagmar. "Not *now*. It's *much* too late for killing children *now*. Why, it's nearly one a.m.! No, there'll be plenty of time in the morning. For now let's all get a good, refreshing night's sleep."

CHAPTER 11

A Desperate Bid for Freedom

The Onts locked Cheyenne and Wally up in their separate bedrooms with the oak dressers, the puffy pillows, and the colorful quilts. Then they put three padlocks on each of the doors so the twins couldn't get out. Then they went back to bed.

Cheyenne sobbed softly in her room and then decided that by morning the Onts would probably calm down and change their minds about killing them.

Wally cursed loudly in his room. He scolded himself for being careless about his wet shoes and letting the Onts discover he'd been in the basement and for meekly allowing himself to be locked into his bedroom, instead of punching each of them in the stomach like he'd punched Rocco at the orphanage. Not that punching the Onts in the stomach would have done much good, but still . . .

Wally tried to figure out a way to escape.

He went to the door of his bedroom and tested the lock to make sure it wouldn't open. It wouldn't.

He raised the window and tried to see if he could slip between the stainless-steel bars. He couldn't. If both his head and his butt had been two inches thick, he could have done it. They weren't.

He looked closely at the stainless-steel bars to see how they were attached to the window opening. The bars were mounted in a steel frame. The frame was screwed into the window opening with a series of twenty-four steel screws.

Wally went and got the Boy Scout knife his dad had given him before he'd drowned in the Porta Potti. He snapped out the screwdriver blade and tried to unscrew one of the steel screws.

At first the screw wouldn't turn. Then, finally, it did. Wally removed all twenty-four screws in less than ten minutes. He carefully lifted out the bars.

He put his toothbrush, his second pair of underpants, and his Boy Scout knife into his pants pockets. And then, with a last look at what would have been a really great room if it weren't owned by giant ants who were breeding a race of super-ants to enslave humans and take over Earth, he crawled through the window.

When Cheyenne first caught sight of somebody outside on the ledge, she was so frightened she

almost wet herself. But when she realized who the somebody was, she was thrilled.

"Wally! How did you ever get out of your room?" she squealed.

"*Ssshh!*" he hissed.

She opened the window. Wally showed her his Boy Scout knife with the screwdriver blade. Then he went to work. In another ten minutes he had removed the twenty-four screws from the bars in Cheyenne's window.

He handed Cheyenne the bars. She put them down quietly on the bedroom floor.

"Grab your stuff and let's get out of here," Wally whispered.

Cheyenne took her toothbrush, her second pair of underpants, and Grandma Gloria's salt-and-pepper shaker and joined Wally out on the window ledge.

Following Wally's lead, Cheyenne carefully made her way down the side of the building to the ground, hanging on to the thick vines that climbed the side of the house.

At one point a vine broke, and they almost

fell to the ground, a fall that would have broken their necks. But Wally grabbed on to a drainpipe, and Cheyenne grabbed on to a TV cable, and they didn't fall.

"We made it!" Cheyenne whispered when they reached the ground.

"Now comes the hard part," said Wally softly. "Getting out of Dripping Fang Forest."

"Don't worry, Wally, we'll do it," said Cheyenne.

"Or die trying," said Wally.

"Which way should we go?"

"Well, we came from *that* direction," said Wally, pointing to the left.

The Shluffmuffin twins began carefully picking their way along the trail to the left. It was night and the woods were dark.

The wind whined through the trees, making an eerie noise. From somewhere not far away came the sound of howling.

"What's that?" said Cheyenne.

"Wolves," said Wally. "At least I *hope* it's wolves."

"You *hope* it's wolves?" Cheyenne asked.

"Rather than werewolves," said Wally.

"Oh," said Cheyenne. "Wally, will wolves attack us?"

"Only if they're hungry," said Wally.

"Oh," said Cheyenne.

"Or if their cubs are hungry," said Wally.

"Oh," said Cheyenne.

"Or if they're mad at us," said Wally.

"Oh," said Cheyenne.

"Or if they're scared of us," said Wally.

"Oh," said Cheyenne.

"Or if they think we're scared of *them*," said Wally.

"Wally . . ."

"Or if they have rabies," said Wally.

"Wally, what will we do if they attack us?"

"Bleed," said Wally.

Cheyenne punched Wally in the arm. "Wally, be serious."

"I *am* serious," he said. "Bleeding is serious."

Just then Cheyenne saw something.

"Wally, what's that?" she whispered.

"What's what?"

"Ahead of us. In the underbrush there. On the right side of the trail." She pointed. "That long, fat glowing thing."

CHAPTER 12

Please Don't Eat the Feet

Wally looked where Cheyenne was pointing.

"It's a long, fat glowing thing," said Wally.

"It's really long," she whispered. "And it's . . . moving toward us."

As the twins watched, the long, fat glowing thing in the underbrush moved closer and closer to them.

"Uh-oh," said Wally.

"What?"

"Do you remember the cab driver telling us the reasons he wouldn't go into Dripping Fang Forest?" Wally asked.

"Sort of."

"Do you remember him saying anything about slimy gray ten-foot-long giant slugs that glow in the dark, attach themselves to your legs, and suck the feet right off your ankles?" Wally asked.

"Sort of," Cheyenne whispered.

As the twins watched, fascinated, a strange thing happened. The long, fat glowing thing suddenly got skinnier, and longer at both ends. A lot longer. Then the two ends of the long

glowing thing began to surround them on both sides.

"Run, Cheyenne, run!" Wally shouted. "Run for your life!"

Wally took off down the trail in the opposite direction of the giant slug. Cheyenne was right behind him.

The giant slug slithered after them.

"Don't worry," Cheyenne called out to her brother, puffing as she ran. "Slugs can't . . . travel fast at all!"

"How do you . . . know that?" Wally puffed.

"At the orphanage . . . when you were . . . learning the *A*'s . . . I had the *S*'s," she answered. "*Slug* was . . . one of my words . . . And they can't . . . travel fast . . . at all."

Wally looked over his shoulder.

"Well, this one . . . hasn't . . . heard that," Wally puffed.

Cheyenne looked over her shoulder. The giant slug was not only keeping up with them, it was pulling ahead!

"Oh no!" Cheyenne cried.

Then, because she was looking over her shoulder and not where she was going, Cheyenne tripped and fell on her face.

The giant slug moved in on her feet. It began eating her left shoe.

"Help!" screamed Cheyenne.

Wally opened his Boy Scout knife, but try as he might, all he could get out was the screwdriver blade.

He rushed toward the giant slug with it.

"Is that supposed to scare me?" asked the giant slug. "A screwdriver?"

"Stop eating my sister's foot!" Wally shouted. "Stop that right this minute!"

"Why should I stop?" asked the giant slug.

"Because. That's my *sister*," said Wally. "You have no right to eat her feet."

"I do *so* have the right to eat her feet," said the giant slug. "Orphan feet are delicious. What does she need feet for, anyway? Look at me. *I* don't have any feet. I don't *need* feet. Is she supposed to be better than me or what?"

Cheyenne unscrewed the top from Grandma

Gloria's salt-and-pepper shaker and poured all the salt out onto the giant slug.

"YIKES!" shouted the giant slug. "SALT!"

"Way to go, Cheyenne!" yelled Wally.

"OW! OW! OW! OW! OW!" shouted the giant slug. "WHAT ARE YOU TRYING TO DO, KILL ME?"

"Yes, of *course* I'm trying to kill you," said Cheyenne.

"But WHY?" demanded the giant slug. "Ow-ow-ow-ow-ow-ow! What have I ever done to deserve that?"

"You were trying to eat my feet off," Cheyenne explained.

"So what?" said the giant slug. "BOY, that smarts!"

"So are you going to die now?" Cheyenne asked.

"Die?" said the giant slug. "No, I'm certainly not going to die. Thanks to you, I'm going to be in a lot of pain, though. OW! But don't worry about me. I'll take a hot bath and two aspirin, and I'll be all hunky-dory in the morning."

The giant slug began slithering away.

"I read that salt kills slugs!" Cheyenne shouted. "How come you're not dead?"

"Don't believe—OW!—everything you read!" answered the giant slug, and it disappeared into the underbrush.

Cheyenne took a deep breath and let it out.

"Whew!" she cried.

"That was amazing!" said Wally. "You were amazing, Cheyenne! I am really impressed."

"Thank you," she said.

"That whole salt thing," said Wally. "You remembered that from the encyclopedia?"

"Just like you with the ants," she said.

"I guess we really have to thank Hortense Jolly for making us spend all that time studying the encyclopedia," said Wally.

"Hortense Jolly," said Cheyenne. "I never used to like old Hortense, but she wasn't all that bad."

"No, not really," said Wally. "Not compared to the Onts."

"You know something? I always felt old Hortense kind of liked us," said Cheyenne.

"And she never threatened to kill us," said Wally. "I do like *that* about her."

"Yes," said Cheyenne. "Hey. Would we ever want to go back to Jolly Days?"

"I don't know," said Wally. "We'll see."

"You mean, first we'll see if anybody wants to adopt us?"

Somewhere nearby a wolf howled disturbingly.

"I mean, first we'll see if we can get out of Dripping Fang Forest alive," said Wally.

CHAPTER 13

Conversations with Wolves

As Wally and Cheyenne made their way along the trail they hoped would lead them out of the forest, a chill wind began to sing through the trees. Cheyenne shivered, hugged herself for warmth, and wished she owned a sweater.

They heard more howling. Howling and growling. Then they began to see eyes. Many pairs of eyes glowing red in the dark all around them.

"Wally, look at all those eyes," whispered Cheyenne. "Are they what I think they are?"

"That depends on what you think they are," said Wally. "If you think they're man-eating wolves, they're what you think they are."

Now they could make out large gray shapes

in the gloom. The large gray shapes began forming a circle around them.

Just ahead on the left was a little house, white with dark wooden beams framing the front. The twins rushed to the house and banged loudly on the door.

As the wolves slowly closed in on them, snuffling and growling, the door of the house swung open. A kind-looking little bald man, wearing blue silk pajamas, a blue silk robe, and gold-rimmed glasses, stood in the doorway.

"May I help you?" asked the little man.

"Please," begged Wally, "may we come inside?"

"Well," said the little man with a frowning smile, looking at his watch, "it *is* a bit late . . ."

"We'd appreciate it so much if we could come inside, sir," said Cheyenne. "We're orphans who are cold and tired and lost and . . ."

". . . and about to have our throats torn out by man-eating wolves," said Wally.

"My, my," said the little man. "Well then, do come in for a moment."

Wally and Cheyenne rushed inside and slammed the door behind them.

The house was warm and cozy. A fire crackled and popped in the fireplace. There was the pleasant smell of woodsmoke. Instead of chairs and sofas, there were huge net hammocks stretched across the room.

"Oh, I *love* your house," said Cheyenne, trying hard not to sneeze. "It's so cozy."

"Thank you. We love it, too," said the little man. He spoke in a calm voice with a British accent. "Allow me to introduce myself. I am Professor Edgar Spydelle. Who are you?"

"We're the Shluffmuffin twins, Cheyenne and Wally," said Wally.

"Pleased to meet you," said the professor. "And by the way, you needn't fear the wolves. Wolves are good creatures, very good. Very loyal. They mate for life, did you know that? That's better than most humans. And wolves have such warm, loving relationships with their little ones. The entire wolf pack cares for each and

every pup. The only bad wolves, in fact, are those that speak."

"Really?" said Cheyenne.

"Yes," said Professor Spydelle. "Unfortunately, all the wolves in Dripping Fang Forest speak."

There was a knock on the door.

"Who is it?" asked the professor.

"May we come inside and chat?" called a raspy voice.

"It's the wolves," the professor whispered to the children, frowning and shaking his head.

The twins shuddered.

"It's a bit late for chatting just now, I'm afraid," the professor answered.

"Really?" called the wolf. "How come it wasn't too late for the boy and girl?"

The professor chuckled, ignoring the wolf's question. "Would you children like something to eat or drink?" he asked. "Tea and gingersnaps perhaps?"

"Tea and gingersnaps, whatever those are, would be great!" said Cheyenne.

"Excellent," said the professor. "I'll ask my wife. Shirley! Some tea and gingersnaps for our guests, please?"

"How come it wasn't too late for the boy and girl?" called the wolf.

"Just ignore him," the professor whispered. "So tell me. What are you children doing out in the forest at so late an hour?"

Wally and Cheyenne looked at each other.

"We just came from Mandible House," said Cheyenne. "Do you know Dagmar and Hedy Mandible?"

"Mandible, Mandible. *Mmm,* the name is a familiar one," said the professor, "but I fear I can't place it just now. Are they friends of yours?"

"No, no," said Wally. "They were thinking of adopting us, but then we discovered they were, you know, giant ants."

The professor's eyebrows climbed his forehead.

"My word! Are you serious?"

"Very serious," said Wally.

"Giant ants," said the professor, shaking his head. "How marvelous!"

"'Marvelous'?" Cheyenne repeated, a puzzled expression on her face.

"Why is that marvelous?" asked Wally.

"You know what *I* think?" called the wolf. "I think you want to eat those children yourself."

"Don't pay him any mind," the professor whispered. "At this time of night, wolves will say most anything."

Wally looked at the professor uneasily, wondering if what the wolf said could be true.

"Selfish pig!" called the wolf. "What about sharing?"

The professor rolled his eyes and smiled.

"Do tell me more about these giant ants of yours," he said. "I have a professional interest, you see. I happen to be head of the bug department at the Cincinnati Museum of Natural History and Science."

"Well," said Wally, "the Onts' basement is filled with hundreds of slimy ant larvae. They're

106

breeding a race of super-ants to take over Earth and end civilization as we know it. We were their prisoners, but we managed to escape."

"You poor dears," said the professor. He clucked his tongue and frowned. "Where will you go now?"

"Back to the Jolly Days Orphanage, I guess," said Wally. "But it's too dangerous to go into the forest until it gets light out. Can we please stay here till morning?"

"Absolutely," said Edgar. "You can curl up in the hammocks while you're waiting for your tea and gingersnaps. Speaking of which, why don't I just go and see how Shirley is coming with those? Make yourself comfortable, children. Use the phone if you like. Feel free to make any calls within the greater Cincinnati area."

The professor left to see about the tea and gingersnaps.

"I like him," said Cheyenne. "He seems so kind. Do you like him?"

"You heard what the wolf said," Wally answered. "Maybe he just wants to eat us himself."

"Oh, Wally, you think everybody wants to eat us," said Cheyenne. "I think he's sweet. Now listen, we know he has a wife. He didn't mention having any children, did he?"

"No, he didn't," said Wally. "Why?"

"Well, if we're very well-behaved, and if I don't sneeze too much, and if—Ah-CHOO!—they don't mind the smell of your feet, then maybe they'd adopt us."

"Before or after they eat us?" said Wally. He went to the phone and picked up the receiver. "I'm going to call Hortense Jolly. See if she'll hide us for a while."

Wally dialed the number of Jolly Days. After thirty-four rings, somebody answered.

"Hullo?" said a voice grumpy with sleep.

"Sorry to wake you, Miss Jolly. It's Wally Shluffmuffin. Cheyenne and I are in trouble, Miss Jolly. Big trouble."

"Wally?" said the voice, losing its grumpiness. "What's the trouble, dear?"

"Well, we ran away from the Mandible

sisters," said Wally. "We barely escaped with our lives. They're giant ants, Miss Jolly! They're breeding a race of super-ants that will eventually make slaves out of the human race and end life on Earth as we know it."

"You ran away from the Mandible sisters?" Hortense repeated. "But, Wally, you mustn't. If you run away, dear, we'll never get our six hundred dollars. You wouldn't want that to happen, would you? No, of course not. We're all partners here at Jolly Days. We're all members of the Jolly Days Team. You must go back to the Mandibles."

"Didn't you hear what I said, Miss Jolly? *The Mandibles are giant ants!* They're breeding a race of super-ants that will eventually make slaves out of the human race and end life on Earth as we know it! When we found out, they decided to kill us tomorrow morning!"

"What makes you think that?" asked Hortense Jolly.

"Because they said, 'We're planning to kill

you tomorrow morning.' Miss Jolly, we can't go back to the Mandibles and we have no place to hide. Can we come back to Jolly Days?"

Hortense Jolly sighed.

"Oh well, I suppose so."

"Good," said Wally. "Thank you, Miss Jolly. We'll be there tomorrow for breakfast."

"The tea and gingersnaps are nearly ready, dear," said Shirley.

The first thing you noticed about Shirley was her legs. Not because they were very long and very hairy but because there were eight of them sticking out of her blue silk pajamas. The next thing you noticed about Shirley were her lovely black eyes. There were eight of those as well. Shirley was a spider quite a bit bigger than her husband.

"You're going to love these children," said the professor. "Their names are Wally and Cheyenne Shluffmuffin. Seems the Mandible sisters wanted to adopt them. They live not far from here, the Mandibles. Do you know the Mandibles, dear?"

"They're humans?"

"*Mmm*, no," the professor answered. "Giant ants, actually. Frightened those poor kids out of their wits. Seems the Mandibles are breeding hundreds of little super-ant larvae in their basement."

"*Larvae!*" Shirley sighed. "Oh, Edgar, I would *so* love hundreds of little larvae in *our* basement."

"But, sweetheart, you know what would happen if we tried to have children."

"Yes, yes, dear, I know." She sighed, pouring tea into little cups.

They both knew what would happen. She would have to eat him. Nothing personal, it was just what female spiders did to their partners after they mated. She would miss Edgar terribly, but just think of all those adorable little spiderlings!

Edgar Spydelle loved his wife. Loved the soft

silky pajamas she spun for them to wear. Loved the way she prepared their food, injecting the meat with her saliva and turning it into a tasty jelly. He just didn't want to have children with her.

"Edgar, dear," said Shirley, "before I take the tea out to the children, shouldn't you prepare them for my appearance?"

"Oh, I don't think that will be necessary, sweetheart. It's only giant ants that frighten them."

"But I do feel you ought to warn them, anyway," she insisted. "Especially after the bad experience they had with the Mandibles."

"Whatever you say, darling."

Edgar came out of the kitchen.

"Tea is ready, children," he said. "But before Shirley brings it out here, I should prepare you for her, uh, somewhat unusual appearance."

"What do you mean?" asked Cheyenne.

"Well, for one thing, she's rather large," said the professor. "For another thing, she's quite hairy."

"Oh heck, you don't have to warn us about stuff like that," said Cheyenne. "I'm very comfortable with large hairy women."

"Excellent. And what about you, Wally?"

"I don't have a problem with large hairy women, either," said Wally. "Unless your wife is a giant *ant*, that is. Ha-ha, that was a joke. Your wife isn't a giant ant, is she, Professor?"

"No, no," said the professor. "She is certainly not a giant ant."

"Then there's no problem," said Wally.

"Good," said the professor. "That's just what I told her. Honey?" he called. "You can bring out the tea and gingersnaps now!"

"All right, dear!" Shirley called.

Moments later Shirley scuttled into the living room, carrying a tray with tea and gingersnaps. From the tips of her forelegs to the tips of her hairy hind legs, she was nearly nine feet long.

Cheyenne and Wally stared at Shirley in disbelief. Then, screaming at the top of their lungs, they lunged for the front door.

"*Awww*, Edgar," said Shirley, "I thought you said you were going to prepare them."

"Well, Shirl, I thought I had," said the professor.

"Now what am I going to do with all these lovely gingersnaps?" she asked, pouting.

CHAPTER 14

We Wolves Are Used to Somewhat Better Treatment

The twins shot out of the Spydelles' house like cannonballs.

The wolves were pretty surprised to see them. There were twenty-seven of them in the pack, sitting or lying in the front yard. When Wally and Cheyenne appeared, they stretched their front paws straight out in front of them, raised their butts high into the air, and slowly got to their feet. Their eyes glowed red in the darkness.

"Well, well, well," said the biggest wolf in a low, raspy voice. He was obviously their leader. "Look who's back. You know, I can't tell you how relieved I am to see you kids safe and sound. I was worried sick the Spydelles might eat you."

His voice was definitely the one they'd heard calling to the professor. Wally and Cheyenne were too frightened to answer.

The wolves began slowly closing in on them, taking their time, knowing they had all the time in the world now. A low rumbling noise came out of their throats.

"You know," said the leader of the pack, "the guys and I were pretty hurt that you ran off before without even saying good-bye." He looked over his shoulder at the rest of the wolves. "Weren't we hurt, guys?"

"We *were* hurt, Fred," said one. He also had a low, raspy voice. "As wolves we are frankly used to somewhat better treatment."

"Kids today," said the wolf leader, shaking his head. "They have no manners. They really must be taught better manners or they'll grow up to be totally rude adults. Am I right, guys?"

"You couldn't *be* more right," said another wolf. "Sassy kids turn into sassy adults. It's a national disgrace."

"What I think we ought to do," said the wolf leader, "we ought to teach these kids a lesson in manners."

"This might not be so bad," whispered Cheyenne into her brother's ear. "They really might just want to teach us some manners."

"Yes," said the wolf leader, "I think we need to teach these kids a lesson in manners they won't forget for the rest of their lives. *For the whole five minutes* of the rest of their lives." He chuckled nastily.

"On second thought," whispered Cheyenne, "it might be pretty bad after all."

Wally nodded.

"Do you have any suggestions?" whispered Cheyenne.

"Just . . . do whatever *I* do," Wally answered under his breath.

"What are you going to do?" whispered Cheyenne.

Good question, Wally thought. *What* am *I going to do? Well, if the choice is being eaten by wolves or giant spiders, I choose wolves. It takes less time to have your throat torn out than to be injected with venom and have your insides slowly turned to mush.*

Wally began to growl.

Cheyenne had never heard her brother growl before. It was a low guttural sound, like he was clearing his throat but lasting longer than that and getting louder.

The wolves looked surprised. They had never heard a human growl before.

Then Cheyenne tried it, imitating Wally but finding it easier than she expected because of all the snot that lived in her nose and throat.

The wolves looked at the two growling children, then at each other. They didn't know whether to laugh or be impressed.

"What are you guys doing?" asked the lead wolf uneasily. "Clearing your throats? You got a virus or stuffed-up sinuses?"

Wally's growling grew louder. So did Cheyenne's.

"You know what's better than Sudafed for clearing out the old sinuses?" said the wolf. "Horseradish. Yep, plain old horseradish. Or sitting in a hot steamy sauna."

If you're ever trapped by a bear—Wally remembered from the encyclopedia under the "Animals Attacking Humans Unexpectedly in Dark Forests of Southern Ohio" heading—*sometimes you can outbluff it. It might not attack if it thinks you're not afraid of it.*

Wally took a nervous step in the wolves' direction. So did Cheyenne. A few of the wolves glanced uneasily at them.

"Sounds to me like a virus," said the wolf. "There's a lot of that going around now. What you need to do is drink lots of fluids, rest in bed, and gargle with hot salty water. Oh, and take echinacea, of course."

He's starting to babble, Wally thought. *Maybe we're making him nervous. I heard that if you're ever attacked by a mugger, the best thing to do is act crazy—the one thing muggers can't handle is crazy people.*

121

Wally suddenly changed his growling to crazy, cackling, high-pitched laughter. Cheyenne immediately did the same. They sounded like two hyenas.

All the wolves looked startled. "What's so funny?" asked the lead wolf, but he sounded worried.

Wally took another step in the lead wolf's direction. He was now four feet away. Cheyenne was right beside her brother.

"Hey," said the wolf, "you wouldn't be laughing at *us*, now, would you? Because wolves don't like to be laughed at. No, sir. That's the one thing we don't allow, being laughed at."

Wally took another step in the lead wolf's direction. One of the wolves backed up a few steps, then pretended it had nothing to do with Wally at all. Wally was so close he could see the wolf's long snout, his dripping fangs, his soft wet nose. He could feel the wolf's hot breath on his face, the wolf's hot stinking breath.

I've got his attention now, Wally thought. *He*

doesn't know what to make of me. He looks really con-
fused. Now I've got to do something totally unexpected.
It'll either work or it'll get us killed, but I've got to do
it now.

Wally bit the wolf on the nose.

"Yowtch!" yelled the wolf, grabbing his nose. "What are you *doing*!? Are you *insane*? Are you completely *nutso*?" He looked over his shoulder at the other wolves. "Did you guys see what this maniac just did to me?" He turned back to Wally. "You are *really* going to get it now, man. You are *so* dead, it isn't even funny."

Three wolves near the edge of the pack drifted away, pretending to be snapping at fireflies.

Cheyenne took the cover off her salt-and-pepper shaker and threw pepper in the wolf's face.

"Ah-CHOO!" the wolf shouted. "What is *wrong* with you kids? Don't you realize who you're *dealing* with here? We're ferocious man-eating wolves. We eat children the way you eat

Mallomars. Do you have any *idea* what we're going to do to you now?"

The lead wolf looked over his shoulder at the members of his pack.

"Just out of curiosity, are you guys behind me here?"

Six of the wolves cleared their throats and scratched their bellies and looked really uncomfortable.

"Any other night of the week, Fred," said one of the wolves, "I'd be right beside you, tearing out throats, but I just realized my wife expected me back in the den twenty minutes ago. I really gotta run." He turned and trotted off into the forest.

"Oh boy," said another wolf, "would you look at the time? I had no idea how late it is. I gotta run, too. Sorry, Fred." He trotted off into the forest as well.

"Whew!" said a third wolf. "What could I be *thinking*, staying out this late? My wife is going to tear my throat out for *sure*. See you tomorrow, Fred." He followed the others into the woods. The remaining wolves slunk away into the darkness, bellies so low they rubbed the ground.

The wolf leader turned back to Wally and Cheyenne.

"Normally, for what you two just did to me, I'd tear your throats out myself," he said. "You're just lucky I pulled a jaw muscle, tearing out a bunch of throats on Thursday. If I tore yours out now, I wouldn't be able to howl for a week."

Wally and Cheyenne began growling again.

"So what I'm going to do, I'm going to let you off easy this time," said the wolf. "But try anything like this again and, man, you are *really* going to get it."

The wolf leader turned around and trotted off after the rest of his disappearing pack.

Cheyenne and Wally watched them go.

"I can't believe we scared off an entire pack of man-eating wolves," said Wally.

"I can't believe you bit a wolf on the nose,"

said Cheyenne. "Where did you ever get the guts to do that?"

"I don't know," said Wally. "It just seemed like a good idea at the time. Where did you ever get the guts to throw pepper in his face?"

"Same place," said Cheyenne. "You know what I think?"

"What?"

"I think we're learning how to handle ourselves pretty well against scary things."

"Well, we're okay against man-eating wolves, I guess," Wally admitted.

"And against giant glowing slugs that eat orphans' feet," said Cheyenne.

"Right," said Wally.

"And against bullies who try and stick us with nasty nicknames."

"I guess so," said Wally. "But we're still not too good against giant ants, giant spiders, or greedy orphanage owners."

"But three out of six isn't bad," said Cheyenne.

Wally chuckled in spite of himself.

"Well, it's a start," he said.

Cheyenne giggled. She hugged him.

And then together they headed out of inky black Dripping Fang Forest.

What's Next for the Shluffmuffin Twins?

Will Wally and Cheyenne get out of the forest without being attacked by something even more disturbing than gigantic slugs, man-eating wolves, or enormous spiders who make tea and gingersnaps?

Have we seen the last of Edgar and Shirley Spydelle, or will they become major characters in this series? (Do you honestly think we'd go to all the trouble of thinking up something as gross as a professor who's married to an enormous spider and *not* bring them back as continuing characters?)

Will Cheyenne and Wally find safety at Jolly

Days, or will Hortense betray their trust and heartlessly double-cross them?

What of the Onts' master plan to breed a race of super-ants, take over mankind, and end life on Earth as we know it? What of that, eh?

And, hey, what about that zombie who drags himself through the swamps, singing "Itsy Bitsy Spider"? Who the heck is he, anyway, and how will he forever change the lives of our friends the Shluffmuffins?

You seriously can*not* afford to miss the Shluffmuffins' next heart-pounding, stomach-churning adventure—Secrets of Dripping Fang, Book Two: *Treachery and Betrayal at Jolly Days.*

DAN GREENBURG writes the popular Zack Files series for kids and has also written many bestselling books for grown-ups. His sixty-six books have been translated into twenty languages. To research his writing, Dan has worked with N.Y. firefighters and homicide cops, searched for the Loch Ness monster, flown upside down in an open-cockpit plane, taken part in voodoo ceremonies in Haiti, and disciplined tigers on a Texas ranch. He has not, however, personally encountered any zombies or glowing slugs—at least not yet. Dan lives north of New York with wife Judith, son Zack, and many cats.

SCOTT M. FISCHER glided through high school doing extra-credit art assignments for math teachers, which is kinda boring stuff to draw. Next he went to art school, where he learned to paint even more boring things—like flower vases. However, he swears that since then he has drawn nothing but cool stuff—like oozy, drooling monsters, treacherous villains, and the occasional flower vase ... that has fangs and eats flowers for breakfast!